To all the children who have become new friends with Bear.

Thank you for reading my books!

– KW

For Boo – I love you

– JC

SIMON AND SCHUSTER
First published in Great Britain in 2006 by Simon & Schuster UK Ltd
1st Floor, 222 Gray's Inn Road, London, WC1X 8HB
A CBS COMPANY

This edition published in 2012 for Index Books

Originally published in 2006 by Margaret K. McElderry Books,
an imprint of Simon & Schuster Children's Publishing Division, New York.

Text copyright © 2006 by Karma Wilson
Illustrations copyright © 2006 Jane Chapman
All rights reserved.

The rights of Karma Wilson and Jane Chapman to be identified as the author and illustrator of this work
have been asserted by them in accordance with the Copyright, Designs and Patents Act, 1988

All rights reserved including the right of reproduction in whole or in part in any form.

Book design by Ann Bobco.
The text for this book is set in Adobe Caslon.
The illustrations are rendered in acrylic paint.

A CIP catalogue record for this book is available from the British Library upon request.

ISBN: 978-0-85707-672-4

Printed in China

1 3 5 7 9 10 8 6 4 2

Bear's New Friend

Karma Wilson

illustrations by Jane Chapman

SIMON AND SCHUSTER

London   New York   Sydney

*I*n the woods, in the sun,
on a hot summer day,
Bear feels an itching
to head out and play.

He goes to find Mouse,
his littlest friend.
But just as big Bear
heads round the bend . . .

. . . there's a clatter in the tree!
Oh, what could it be?
And the bear
              asks,
                      "Who?"

Bear calls, "Is that Mouse
who hides in the tree?"
But Mouse scurries up
and squeaks, "It's not me!"

Bear scratches his head.
"Who's hiding up there?"
Mouse shrugs his shoulders.
"Perhaps it is Hare?"

Mouse starts to shout, "Come out, friend, come out!"
And the bear
asks,
"Who?"

Nobody answers.
"Who is it?" asks Bear.
They peek in the tree,
but nobody's there!

Bear cries, "No one's here!
But where did they go?"
Then Hare hops along
and says, "Howdy-ho!"

"Something sped past, going fast, fast, fast!"

And the bear
asks,
"Who?"

Hare says, "Let's go follow,
to see what we see."
Bear says, "Is it Badger?
Who else could it be?"

But there by a log
with Gopher and Mole,
Badger is peering
into a deep hole.

ok if you dare! There's someone down there!"

And the bear
asks, "Who?"

Bear says, "It's not us!
But who is it then?"
"I know!" says Badger.
"It's Raven or Wren."

But Raven and Wren
flap down from the sky.
"We saw all our friends
and thought we'd fly by."

Up from the ground comes a rustling sound.
And the bear
asks,
"WHO?"

"Who are you down there?
Who is it, I say?
Why stay in that hole?
Why hide the whole day?

"Why don't you like us?
WHY, WHY, WHY?"
Then a trembling voice says,
"Because – I am shy."

Two eyes peek-a-boo and the voice says, "Who?"
And the bear
says,
"Hi!"

"I'm Bear. Howdy-ho!
That's Mouse and that's Hare.
And Gopher and Mole
are standing right there.

Next to those bushes
sit Raven and Wren.
Come swimming with us
in the pool by the glen!

"Please do not hide. Come on outside."

Then . . .

. . . an owl says,

"Hello, I'm Owl.
And I'm sorry I hid.
I'm just a bit bashful,
and that's why I did."

Bear says, "Hello, friend!"
"Come on," cries Mole.
And they all scamper off
to the old swimming hole.

They splash and have fun in the hot summer sun ...

with Bear's
new
friend.